SEE ME DIG

by Paul Meisel

I Like to Read®

Holiday House / New York

For Cheryl.
And for Rusty, our blind Brittany spaniel,
who likes to dig.

I LIKE TO READ is a registered trademark of Holiday House, Inc.

Copyright © 2013 by Paul Meisel
All Rights Reserved
HOLIDAY HOUSE is registered in the U.S. Patent and Trademark Office.
Printed and Bound in June 2013 at Tien Wah Press, Johor Bahru, Johor, Malaysia.
The text typeface is Report School.
The artwork was executed in pen and ink, acrylic, pencil,
and watercolor on Waterford watercolor paper.
www.holidayhouse.com

3 5 7 9 10 8 6 4 2

Library of Congress Cataloging-in-Publication Data
Meisel, Paul.
See me dig / by Paul Meisel. — 1st ed.
p. cm. — (I like to read)
Companion book to See me run.
Summary: A group of dogs that loves to dig has a fun-filled day
of making mischief in this easy-to-read story.
ISBN 978-0-8234-2743-7 (hardcover)
[1. Dogs—Fiction.] I. Title.
PZ7.M5158752Sdm 2013
[E]—dc23
2012016549

See me dig.
I like to dig.

We all like to dig.
We dig and dig.

Oh, no! They are mad.

We run away.

We can dig here.

What is this?

It is a box.

We tug and tug and tug.

Oh, no!
They are mad.

We run and run.

We must stop them.
I will be brave.

Woof!

Woof! Woof!
See them go.
I am a hero.

He likes to dig too.

Now we dig some more!